chaos

Sandra,

Hope you enjoy the book!

Lots of love,

Chloë

chaos

chloe binns

To the ones who made it to after

STORM

You are thunder and lightning; the storm people chase. They'll never catch you, no one ever will. They can't get enough of you, awestruck by your presence, you ignite passion in their souls. You radiate beauty. Remember that. Next time you feel the doubts creeping in, the ones which haunt the crevasses of you skeleton, run at them head first. Shatter them into a million insignificant pieces. You are profound and you will survive. It's built into your core, that incessant ability to stand up every single damn time. And stand up fighting.

They will try everything to push you into oblivion but they don't know that you are oblivion; you are a whirlwind of chaos. You can't live by their standards, by their requests; you have to retain your wild. The wildness which came from survival. You thrive on the outstanding because it makes you feel alive, it keeps your mind burning and awake. Your energy is addictive, and you astonish your spectators. Never lose your momentum, it drives them into the ground, buries them and allows you to run undisciplined. You are infinite, inconceivable magic.

Don't ever give them what they want, give them hell.

ABLAZE

You don't react to anything. Your fuse isn't short. But you feel the frustration engulfing you. You watch as people walk all over the body you once inhabited, not realising that you no longer live there. You're a ghost now, floating above and watching. Waiting. You see now what you wish you'd known all along. You are tormented by hindsight. And all the while you're burning inside, a fire so powerful it devours you. But you know that soon enough you won't be the only one burning. You bide you time, until you feel yourself spill over into the world.

You set the sky ablaze with a flare so bright it's excruciating to look at. But you feel no shame, because even alight you know you're still mesmerising. So you burn, and see their faces as they wonder how it happened, why anyone would set themselves on fire. But little do they know the only thing blazing is an effigy which existed for their pleasure; for their gain. You are astonishingly beautiful and they see that now. As they mourn the loss of someone they wished they hadn't killed. And the guilt rises inside them like the blistering sensation they once inflicted on you. But you've always been rising above, and it's too late for them now.

You may have lit the match, but it was them who spilled the gasoline.

JAW

I watched as you dragged me across the floor, too
tired to scream but too in love to drag myself out. As
you kicked me once but loved me twice as hard. As
you held my face against the stone but held your
hands against my heart.

I cried, as you screamed how pathetic I was but how
pathetically in love with me you were. As you looked
at me with disgust, but you were the only one looking
at all. As you held the lighter against my skin until it
burned your love into my veins, your persistent
reminder that your love for me burned brightest.

I screamed, as you held me under water, but over
your dead body would you ever love me less. As you
threw me brutally, but caught me softly. As the glass
broke my skull, but I deserved it because I was
breaking your heart.

I think a lot about the way your fist felt as it
connected with my jaw. It feels a lot like my heart,
now that you're gone.

EDGE

Me and you, we wanted to be everything. We grew up dreaming of never growing old. Both of us with a Peter Pan complex and a dream of finding Neverland. We wanted to explore the world without ever having to leave each other's pockets. We believed that the sky was as endless as our love - an infinite mass of stars and galaxies and magic. That even if we stumbled upon the edge of the universe we still wouldn't find the end of our love. We knew time travel was possible, our love spanning the ages. The greatest story ever told was ours and for as long as it left peoples lips, our love would never die. We saw the sun on the darkest of days because we lived above the clouds, without shadows or shade. We thought that the touch of each other was enough to induce miracles.

You and I were never meant for this world.

WANDER

Once you've been broken you become reckless, hyper aware that you have nothing left to lose. You know that trying to pick up the shards of your shattered heart will leave you with cut hands. So you leave them there; splintering, glittering on the floor. You understand that what's broken may never be fixed. You lost your energy trying to pick up everybody else's pieces, helping them glue their hearts back together. But now you realise that there's no one left to help you fix yours.

You wait for the fragmented pieces to become worn and tarnished around the edges, the heavy tide of time wearing them away. You wait for them to become smooth from the consistent torment and abuse. And then you tell yourself you'll pick them up when they can't hurt you anymore. When they've become so raw and brutalised they look like tiny glass tears. Then you tell yourself it'll be safe to pick them up. To slowly put them back together. But you've forgotten that the longer you wait, the further your heart wanders from fitting together in the same way anymore.

UNLOCKING

He was always floating so far above the earth, while
she retained her ever grounded feet. She knew that
he was every star in sky, the entire universe embodied
him, and she ached to feel the weightlessness of the
galaxies he inhabited. He knew, that stars were only
temporary, eventually they burnt out.

He saw knowledge encompassed her, she represented
worldliness, she knew the corners of the earth as
though she'd designed them, and he sought to
conquer his own mind as she had hers. She
understood, that so often ignorance was bliss.

Through admiration they offered one another
balance. They held hands and promised to seize the
world together. She started to slowly float towards
the sky, whilst he gently returned to the earth. He
held her and saw the stars he was crafted from
reflected in her eyes. She embraced him and truly saw
the inner workings of his mind. It had always existed,
it just needing unlocking.

.

CRACK

You let him throw you against the wall. You let your head fracture against the stone. You let him pick you up and throw you again. You choose to remember him picking you up.

You let him remind you that you're worthless. That you would be less than nothing without him. You choose to remember that makes you something.

You let him cut open your soul with his cruel taunts. Kiss you and comment that your lips are dry and cracked. You only remember how his lips still touched yours.

You let him because you know you need each other. Because you don't know how to function without his hands around your neck. Because you know he controls your heartbeat. Because breaking free from him means you may never feel anything again. Because the pain you feel when your body breaks from the impact of his hands still doesn't hurt as much as the pain you felt when the one before left you with a broken heart.

WILD FLOWERS

She wanders aimlessly, hoping something catches her attention, something that will distract her from her mind. She seeks the great unknown, reliant on the prospect it will release her from the shackles from which she has become accustomed. She aches for the relief of having someone sweep the disarray from her skull. Of having a body which resembles life, instead of the entrapment of her decaying corpse. Caught in a cage of her own making, desperately trying to escape.

But the weeds which sprout in her mind, the thorns which threaten to pierce her heart, the brambles which encase her fragile ribs, all grow because she waters them. She waters them with self-hatred, with contempt, with disgust. She encourages their development, before despairing at how relentless they've become. Instead, she should water the parts she finds beautiful, allow the damaged weeds to rot.

She resents her mind, but it is a mesmerising garden of wildflowers.

SUBMERSED

When you hurt someone and they still choose you, they're choosing pain over pleasure. They're choosing you because it is agony to be with you, but its unimaginable to be without you. These are the people who are truly lost, who are so fragile and broken they don't know how to swim up to the surface and prevent themselves from drowning. We don't drown because we can't breathe, we drown because we can't breathe water.

They're submersed in the very thing which is killing them - agonisingly, painfully murdering them. But they would rather die surrounded by you, than learn to swim on their own. They're waiting for you to rescue them, to pull them up to the air alongside you, but instead they're kicking against the tide. Against the ripples you're sending their way because you're so busy kicking yourself towards the oxygen. Leaving them forgotten, and anchored to the seabed.

Either they kick hard enough to push free or they become buried in a watery grave. The one you dug for them.

BRUISING

Because you breakdown and feel the pure agony of heartbreak as it coarse's through your entire body. People lie when they tell you its numbing, it isn't. It consumes every nerve of your body with pure, unfiltered pain. It stops your breath until you choke without oxygen and your lungs turn black from bruising. It catches you completely off guard, blindsiding you with a brutal stab wound but no one can see you bleeding out, hear you crying out. It chooses the cruelest times to remind you that your heart is no longer whole, just at the moment when you think you can feel it beating again. And just as you exhale a sigh of relief that the worst is over, you'll be dragged back into the realm of all-encompassing anguish. There's no cure, there's no help, there's no escape. Just a black hole of emptiness, and you're burning hope that one day maybe you won't wake up and feel as though you're already dead. But a part of you did die. Maybe it's a part you'll learn you never needed.

MAP

And I think that at some point I may have to accept that I will always be in some kind of love with you. It won't always be this painful or this consuming but a small part of me will always be with the thought of you. Maybe it's hard to accept now, because hearing your voice could bring me to tears and seeing your face would dismantle me, but maybe one day I'll be grateful to hold onto the splinters I have left. The sharp edges of our shared history cuts me to ribbons now but it won't always.

Eventually, the cuts will become scars, white and smooth on my skin and someone else will trace their finger down them and wonder how someone could suffer this much pain and survive. They'll become a map of my history, some from you and many from others. I will follow them towards unharmed skin, still waiting to be written on. Whilst the scars fade and symphonize with the rest of me, they will always show up, a little bit lighter, a little bit more pronounced.

They're beautiful. But there will be no more inflicted by you.

ENOUGH

And when things get really bad, the nights when the world is ending and you've convinced yourself the sun will never rise. Remember it was real. It may have been heart wrenchingly sad, it may have broken you down in a thousand different ways but never forget that it was all real. The fingertips that touched your face and traced the curve of your spine. The eyes which stared directly into your soul and back into the universe. The voice which made you whole for once and feel as though poetry was as easy as exhaling. The smell which lingers on your favourite sweater, his, yours, his, ours. It was all real. It all meant something. And it changed the world. For better or for worse, history was made. You don't have to remember, or reminisce, or romanticise.

You just have to know that when it gets hard, you two changed the world. And maybe, just maybe, that's enough.

ONES

This is for the ones who dream of stranger worlds. Who look into the night sky and swear they can see figures dancing on the rings of Saturn. Who fall asleep each night drifting endlessly on weightless pink clouds, dreaming in undiscovered colours. For the ones who believe the tops of trees hold passages to lands in the sky, that the wind carries secrets to those who choose to listen, and with a long enough ladder you could pluck a star from the sky. For those who daydream about islands in the ocean, with mystical creatures and magical people. The ones who fly through the forests with fairies, swim the seas with mermaids and sprinkle stardust from the clouds. This is for the ones who dream of sitting on the moon, of dipping their toes into blue pools and falling in love with the sun.

For the ones who believe in magic.

BRAVE

She waits for him to take a step in the wrong direction. To veer slightly off her carefully planned course. She extracts enjoyment from his wrongdoing, channeling the sharp stab she feels in her chest. Each time she feels the knife of resentment pierce her heart, she smiles. She feeds on the twisted nature of their relationship. Before, she would curl up, wait for him to tread his heavy footsteps all over her fragile body, and her vulnerability would take over. But no more. Before, she would beg for his touch across her skin, his breath on her cheek and feel rejection sweep across her world without it. But no more.

Now, she stores his jibes and recognises her position of power. She manipulates each situation to her advantage. Understanding that with each wrong footing she regains another fraction of control. It's the long game. But it's worth it. To see the look on his face as he realises he lost her all over again. She seeks the satisfaction of holding his broken heart in her hands. She aches to see his eyes lose their glimmer. She's lost sight of how sick she's become, a warped image of the once loving girl. But she was weak, she was taken advantage of, she was a mess. And now she'll laugh as she tightens her fingers around his neck, the air leaves his body and light disappears from his world.

Revenge is for the brave.

THOUSAND

It will always feel like torture when you leave him, it will rip you into a thousand pieces and you will never collect them all in the same way again. But there are infinite ways to rearrange your fragments and you're yet to find the most beautiful.

BEFORE

The time before you. Before you laid your eyes on me, and they came to rest. I don't remember the last breath I took before you, but I wish I did. I would savour it. Its intoxicating purity. When my mind was blank of your face and I didn't have to scrub myself clean every night to try and remove the feel of your fingertips from my skin. I resent lying in our bed, the gut wrenching realisation that when you left, you took sleep with you. When I could fall asleep, without your arms around me and your fingers drawing intricate patterns on my back, in my hair, willing me to dream sweetly.

I wish I could look into the sky, and not know that you lie under the same stars, that we're both staring at the same moon. I want so badly to not know you. To have never known you. To have never felt the high, because the low is harrowing.

I wish there was just me. That there had never been a you.

UNWAVERING

Thank you. For everything. For showing me that the world is so much bigger than my own, the oceans deeper, the sky endless. For teaching me that terror is temporary, but that not everything has to be. For not trying to save me, but holding my hand as I tried to save myself. For opening my eyes to the prospect that some things are infinite and that intertwining your soul with someone doesn't have to be dangerously frightening. It can be fulfilling and effortless and so beautiful. For understanding my imperfections without question, without critique, without acknowledgment. For not even seeing them as flaws, but embracing them as the stones which build my frame. For relentlessly trying to infiltrate my heart.

For your unwavering honesty in the face of adversity, and your ability to see the stars buried deep in the depths of my eyes. Combining our faults, our mistakes, our insecurities and sharing the burden. For helping me to believe in a future which I couldn't comprehend existed. For reminding me that storms are only present to wash us clean. For assuring me that beauty radiates from my core, when all I can see is fog. For utterly immersing yourself in our world, the one you created for us.

Quite simply, for loving me.

LASH

You lash out. You translate your words to thunder and your actions to lightening. You embody fear but translate fierceness. You refuse to let them see you suffer so you fight. You fight so hard and it's admirable. But eventually you tire. You become exhausted with having to be so reckless.

You've spent so long battling, you hadn't realised that the worst scars are the ones you've inflicted on yourself. You realise that what you thought was sweat from exertion are the tears flowing down your own face. For the first time, you see yourself clearly. You see what they pushed you to become, but you can't be that anymore. You can't keep lashing out when the only damage is you. You have to rest. You have to be vulnerable.

The struggle makes you strong, but the rest makes you realise.

EMBERS

They believe that you are inexplicably astonishing. That you wake up each day and the glint in your eye is never dim. It's bright and powerful and radiant. You throw kindness into the universe and simply open your umbrella when all that you receive in return is a rain cloud. You choose to see the storm for its beauty, for its power. You admire it's fierceness and refuse to cower in its presence. You dance in the embers of its misery. You take the sadness from the souls of those you love and carry them on your shoulders to relieve them of the pressure.

But you're trying to forget that it's all a façade. That each day you have to try harder to keep your mask in place. That you choose to ignore that your sunshine smile is slowly thawing to reveal the harsh winter which rages below. That your reason for never giving up is because you've already invested so much that walking away with nothing means you've failed again. And you're so tired from carrying around the heaviness of despair.

Everyone believes that you're unbreakable, but you know that's easy when there's nothing left to break.

DECEIT

The lies swallow you whole. They engulf you until you believe that all of the words spoken are true. You trust each sound and each movement until you mirror them yourself. You hear the same lies spill from your own mouth as you repeat them to anyone who will listen. Your tongue black but your intentions white.

You believe your own manipulated truth because it's all you've ever been told. The entire sphere in which you orbit becomes an unfathomable sequence of deceptions. It's not your fault though, how could you know any different? You read between the lines.

You're the lie.

PARALYSING

Sometimes the idea of lost love can be more paralysing than the affair. Torturing yourself with thoughts of what could have been, until eventually it becomes a distorted figure of something which never existed. Perspective and comprehension become the unseen antagonist. Your pain is not poetic and people will not write novels based on the breaking of your heart. Uncomprehendingly, there are still hearts more broken than yours

You have to forgive yourself. Stop punishing the thoughts which spill from your brain, a puddle of sorrow flowing across the floor. Face towards the light and watch the shadow fall behind you. Learn to walk independently for the first time in so long. Unsteady but solitary. You're flourishing again, blooming into the girl before.

You may not be the girl people write songs about, but you're a chorus of love.

CHANGED

With certainty, I can say that you're not what I want. I know now you're the furthest thing from everything I desire, a memory of torments gone by. There is no love lost, because you were never mine to lose. You were always just out of my reach, a breath from being my own. Which only made it easier to let go. After all, I was the only one holding on.

And then I saw you with her. And I changed my mind.

BATTLESCARS

You will not heal by going back to what broke you. You're just dressing your wounds. Covering them up, whilst allowing the same person to keep hurting you, keep inflicting more and more pain. For a while they make things better, help you fix yourself back up, they lift you up to feeling like you're worth something more than nothing. They help you feel whole again, as though the scars are finally recovering and all that's left is a hazy stain. A battle scar.

But its temporary, it's so fucking fragile.

They will never stop hurting you, and even when they make promises to never lay a vicious finger on you again, they will. Because you can run from your injuries, you can fight against the memories which haunt you, but the jagged lines will forever be etched on your skin, across your mind. Poignant reminders of the hurt they inflicted. And they can never take those away from you. You cannot move forward with someone who broke you so badly. Even after resurrecting all of your pieces, you can still see all of the cracks. And you can only see their face reflected in them. You deserve so much more than hastily constructed, false promises. You have to fucking get out. You have to stop relying on someone who holds the power to continuously break you. There is no shame in having a body covered with battle scars, as long as they're no longer being inflicted.

MAYBE

How do you stop tears falling? How do you carry on with something which breaks your heart every fucking day? How do you breathe when your chest is crushing your lungs and your ribs are piercing your fragile heart? How do you know if love is enough? I can't answer, I can only keep going until I break, because I can't let him go. I can't bear the thought of a moment without him swimming around my mind, diving into the depths of my soul, of us drowning together.

But what happens when these moments become too far and wide. Is giving up before you break, wise or stupid? Does the distance you're willing to push your heart, to the point where it bursts, does it prove your worth? Your value on him, on you, on your togetherness.

I can feel my world crumbling around me but when did I become so dependent, so fucking reliant? Maybe I fell in love with him when when I saw the way he looked at me and I finally saw myself through his eyes. Maybe I could feel the warmth of his heart melting my soul and maybe that's enough. Maybe this all comes down to two people and the love they share being enough. Or maybe I've suffered enough and I can't take the weight dragging me down anymore.

But is love knowing that you're being pulled under and that's ok, because you're drowning together?

QUESTION

And all of those nights we spent lying on your bedroom floor, tracing constellations into my spine, are worthless because you tainted them with your cruelty. The nights we danced in those dingy bars, to some band I don't even remember, but it wasn't important as long as I could hear you singing the words into my ear, are over. You dragged me away from home and left me on the bathroom floor of some club, crying and drunk because I wasn't worthy of you and never would be.

And all I wanted to do is sit a while and ask you every question I never had the chance to. Every question which spun through my mind at 4am, every question which crashed from my fist into the wall, every question which falls in the shape of tears hitting my pillow. But you took that from me, snatched it away, when you left without looking back.

Then I started to remember how pathetic you sounded when you begged me not to leave you. How you couldn't sleep at night with the lights out, because the darkness suffocated you. How much you resented your sober mind. And suddenly I stopped feeling so helpless.

And now the only question I have is whether you drink to forget me or because it hurts too much to remember?

POISONOUS

It's a damn good job you like your girls crazy. Electric
to the touch and poisonous at the tongue. To keep
you on your toes when idleness threatens to cut you
off at the knee. You like them fierce and feral, dirty
handed and filthy minded. Pure bred insanity
coursing through their veins.

It's a damn good job because I'm fucking insane.

THREAD

They used to stand hand in hand. Inseparable. A bond between them so intricate it had weaved its way through each of them inside and out. Stitched together through self-hatred, isolation, anxiety, they sought to ignite a passion for life. She stood and saw her pain reflected in the girl's eyes, and it was comforting. It reassured her that she wasn't alone. She clung to her in order to survive, to see reason in living. And the girl requited this.

Until she could take no more. As she healed herself, she watched helplessly at her futile attempts to take her friend with her. She blamed herself, she vowed to try harder. But eventually she realised, it was never her fault. The girl wallowed in self-pity; she indulged in playing the victim. But only with her.

She watched as the girl flourished with everyone else and crawled back to her for the sympathy she craved. She acquired only the decay and none of the bloom.

In the end, it was her friend who pushed her and watched as she fell. And as she fell, the girl hurled viscous words at her. She screamed of the betrayal, of how she was left behind. It didn't hurt as she fell, she thought it might. The realisation it was her friend who inflicted the final blow didn't come as a shock, she'd been expecting it. She landed and gently started to pick away the threads which attached her to her former shadow.

HAUNT

You'll let them tighten their fingers around your neck because you trust that they won't tighten them further. You let them throw you away because you trust that they'll pick you back up. You feel sickened at the thought of them being anywhere but in your arms and your heart. You ache to feel their touch on your body and your soul and your mind. The holes which once existed inside of you, the ones which gaped and sucked the life from your world are now filled. They filled them. With love.

You agonise over the concept of them leaving you, of the prospect of the space they'll leave behind. Much greater and deeper than before. But you know that a love this big is worth the risk. You'll grasp for each other in the darkness and know that they're there. Even after they're gone, their ghost will haunt you. It will haunt the corners of your mind, the cracks in your soul. You will never be able to escape them. But the thing is, you won't want to.

SHAME

So I flirt with the new guy. Watch his eyes dart to my screen when your name shows up, my eyes on his as I turn it over. Deflect his questions about where I was last night, with who. Never telling him it was you who dropped me off, the same one picking me up the morning after.

You say she's not your girlfriend, but she's not the secret. Her calling you, while you call me, while I'm with him. All asking the same questions to different people, all lying about what it means. We dragged them into our game, but they don't even know they're playing. Two opposing sides, two people in love.

It's just a shame it's not us.

OVERDOSING

We were so busy injecting ourselves with each other, we didn't realise we were dying. Overdosing and dependant. More potent that anything we'd ever taken, and excruciating to give up. A hazy fog of pleasure that burned fast and fierce.

ALIGHT

You have to let it all go. Whether you move forward with him or choose to leave him standing alone you have to push all of it away. You either say how you feel and it fucks everything up or you say nothing and let it fuck you up instead. The only person left hurt is you. You will start to rot from the inside out. And you should always be blossoming. You should be shining so brightly.

So let it out, set your heart free, set your soul alight. And remember, whether you choose to live with or without him doesn't matter, because you will forever be able to live with yourself.

COMPANY

You are completely alone. It's a frighteningly isolating moment when you realise that no one else in the universe can understand the workings of your mind. No one else can relate to every feeling which pulses across your body, or comprehend the currents which coarse through your veins.   It will never matter how much you share or how much you confide or how much you scream. No one truly understands. You are not lonely, you are desolate.

Any company which passes through your life is shallow; a superficial attempt to neglect the knowledge you are companionless throughout your journey. It's a temporary measure to warn away the understanding that you're trapped in the prison of your own mind. The solidarity will kill you eventually, a torturous death where you are cut into ribbons by your own shattered heart.

There is never an escape, no back up plan, no exit route. You're forever trapped in the painfully isolated world you wander through. So many people look through you, look at you, look up to you and yet none of them can see the weight you carry with you. You spend your whole life searching for someone who can read your mind, who you can share your deepest conceptions with.

But no one ever will, not really.

GHOST

We're all inherently made up of the same components. We exist through the same chemical make up, the same design, the same structure. And yet somehow - she was different. Like she was made of something more than the rest of us. A fragment of biology which was completely accidental and yet gave her a purpose beyond anyone else.

I don't believe in magic or in the serendipity of coincidence but she makes me believe in something. Something I can't catch between my fingers or allow to fall off the edge of my tongue. Something which gives hope to the rest of us, something which we will spend our lives chasing after, trying and failing to live up to.

It's impossible to live up to the great expectations of the dead. They're on a pedestal too high to climb and too grounded to topple. Ghosts who live with each of us and follow our thoughts. She was clever you see, she left a little part of herself in each of us making it impossible to move on. She anchored herself within me and now I can feel myself disappearing. Maybe I'm already invisible to everyone but her.

She's laughing at me, as she watches me drown.

PRY

I was so involved in you, that giving up on you felt like I was giving up on myself. I had given every last part of myself to you, to make us work, to make us happy. But when that wasn't enough for you it felt like I wasn't enough either.

I'm exhausted from trying to pry apart the me that existed before you and the me which still doesn't know how to survive without you. I spent so much time putting myself second to you that you started to do the same. I taught you how to put me second.

BLOOD

She knew you, you told her everything about yourself.
Even the parts which felt rotten inside of you; so
disgusted in your choices and so at war with yourself.
A friendship so strong you felt bonded through blood.

But she changed her mind. She decided you weren't
good enough to hold her attention and you watched
as she chose anyone else but you. You heard her voice
tell you that you were sisters but her actions showing
you how little she valued you. She took all of your
most vulnerable emotions and arranged them into a
eulogy she could read back to you. You let her
assassinate you because you were still so wrapped up
in how exposed she told you she was. You still
couldn't bear to hurt her.

You reflect on how she manipulated the situation
which led you into being the villain. She cast you as
the enemy before you agreed to be part of her show
and now you're performing under her direction
without having learnt your lines. A web of lies
weaved cautiously around your neck, waiting for the
drop to end you, ensuring her hands remain clean.

But she forgets that you know her too. That you know
how her mind works as well. And you know the very
things which haunt her thoughts. Things you will
preserve until the time is right.

DRUNK

And here I am again. Drunk and covered in a thin layer of sweat – a mixture of mine, theirs, everyone's. Propped up on the bathroom floor of a bar I don't recognise. And I see each crack in the ceiling as I refuse to look anyone in the eye. They try to pull me up, tell me whatever it is they can help. But they can't. And I hate them because they think my problems are so fucking romantic. My hair plastered to my face as I try to remember the last time I saw yours. I hate my reflection because it looks so much like you.

And all I can remember is how much hate fills my heart. I try to drown it with noise, with drugs, with anything, but it's all so temporary. The only cure is you. But you're not here and I am. Except I don't fucking know where here is anymore. I should stand up, pull myself together, wipe your stain from my mind but you're engrained. A cancer which has enveloped my body and all of the scratching and fighting in the world can't claw you clean away. Because the dark reality is I love you.

It's dangerous because I love you a fuck ton more than myself.

SHIFT

Something's changed. She can feel it in the atmosphere. The wind blows around her differently; it's a shift in the atmosphere. She's not sure she believes in magic anymore, questions her commitment to serendipity. She can't place her finger on exactly what has changed, but she knows. Something deep inside her is telling her it's altered.

Gut feeling. She always pushes it away as illogical, an incessant nagging which fractures her happiness. But what happened last time? When she threw herself in the opposite direction, to try and escape everything she felt inside her. The gentle ticking which kept her sanity intact began to race and she sung louder, more out of tune to quieten it.

But she was right. That tiny part of her, which caused a lump to sit in her throat, caused her bones to feel the chill and ensured sleep deserted her, was right. She swore after last time she would never ignore it again. But even now, she's resisting. Because she doesn't want to believe, it's less painful to ignore. But she can't run forever, she can't sing forever, she can't deceive forever.

ROCKPOOLS

I brought the new you around the places that once belonged to us. A sadistic tour of the wreckage that was us.

I took him to the beach where you kissed me first thing in the morning and last thing at night. Showed him the rock pools like we were discovering them for the first time together. Let him drive my car in the inky darkness, street lamps shining a spotlight on my recklessness. He holds my hand the same way you did, stroking his thumb down the creases of my palm, as the other grips the steering wheel steady and sure. We walked into the forrest and marvelled at carvings in the trees, love immortalised in bark.

I never told him it was our initials he was admiring.

RAFT

Every day is mesmerisingly frightening when you know that you've let your happiness be controlled by someone else. When you remember the depths you can be pulled to, you know how much you never want to drown again but you realise that you never learned to swim while you had the chance. Once upon a time, you allowed yourself to be immersed in the water and just as you were about to kick off and swim out alone you were thrown a life raft.

You're floating and you know that your every movement is supported by a raft and if that ever fails you, you'll be stranded in the middle of the ocean with no hope of being able to get back. Do you try to push yourself closer to shore just in case? Do you jump from the raft and force yourself to swim? Or do you just continue to float, hoping that everything will be ok but live with the knowledge that each day you come closer to being pulled under forever.

STILL

Sometimes, in the quiet, when I think everything has moved on, I remember what he did. The only thing he swore he would never do, the line to never be crossed. And I hurt all over again.

The ache of betrayal never leaves you, never stops clawing at your insides. I chose forgiveness but it's so damn hard. To know someone could decide to hurt you so badly. An apology means nothing when it comes from an empty promise. Because once is a mistake, twice is a punishment for who you are. They knew what it would do to you and they did it anyway. Their selfishness tearing you apart and still, when the world stops, you're the one still standing for them.

BEAUTIFUL

He asked me how a girl so beautiful could be so sad.
I replied, 'because after all this time, you still don't
know me at all'.

BUZZ

Curious though it seems, you miss the buzz. One day, you're driving along, little purpose, fewer worries. Pleasantly aimless. And then it hits you, the cold air slams against your body, pulls the air straight from your lungs. You feel the blood drain from your head and the dizzying rush as a lack of oxygen fails to reach you. You realise you can't hear the buzz. Just silence.

You're so used to hearing it bouncing around your skull, you're deafened by nothing. You feel content, you feel safe, and you feel all-encompassing love. He makes you feel the warmth burning in your heart, one that's reflected in his. Him whispering your name as your eyes slip shut each night.

So familiar is the buzz it leaves you confused. You can't separate whether you're feeling happiness or nothing at all. You struggle with whether the silence is frightening or just unfamiliar. You don't understand because all of those ones before created a buzz in your ears so loud it ricocheted across the universe and back again. It's doubt, self-loathing, insecurity. Don't chase the buzz because it's familiar, because it feels like all of those times before.

The times before were wrong.

The silence is just love.

FRAYED

The nights are warm and stretching. We're here, all of us, under the moonlight. Frayed but euphoric. The atmosphere electric with anticipation for the unknown. We glitter with hopefulness we're too naive to understand. Projecting our futures as far as the early hours. The undercurrent of energy infecting each one of us.

We're too young to be so sad.

RATTLE

Because so little of what we do is clean cut. So few things retain their simple black and white nature for long. The hearts wants what it wants, until it gets it, and then the grey scale of turbulence sets in. Your heart begins to rattle in its cage with insecurity. You fight against the fear and disorientation of trust, trying to determine whether you're self destructing or finally something has clicked.

Are you losing your mind or are you finally opening it up?

You wage an endless war in your mind between the person you fell for and the one they revealed themselves to be. And you become exhausted and disheartened, you no longer have the fire inside it takes to stay strong. You reach out for their hand but each time you flail in the thick air which awaits you.

And again you try to figure out whether they're simply not there or you're so busy waving your hands around you're darting straight past them. And so you still yourself, you force yourself to ask the questions you're frightened to answer.

Is it them or me?

PINKY

You entered my veins and disregarded my safety. Slipped my arm through yours and then the railings. I watched, disembodied, as it snapped. Like your fingers when you needed me to come running. Each mark a token of your love. A gift from your hands, for me only. You bonded us through the bruises that travel down my body, each possessing a story more disturbing than the last.

Pinky promises broken like my fingers.

CASUALTIES

We met by accident, a pure chance we could never have anticipated. Something greater than both us pulled us together, a cosmic twist of fate designed to create a beautiful connection. You and I wrapped in a modern fairy tale, wanting for nothing but the other.

Who could have known something so bright could tarnish so quickly. Empty us both out, leaving us hollow and bitter. A spark extinguished the same way it was lit. Casualties of coincidence.

I wish I could forget you. So I could meet you all over again.

Printed in Great Britain
by Amazon